ROBIN HOOD

PARENT HOOD

D1424192

BBC CHILDREN'S BOOKS

Published by the Penguin Group
Penguin Books Ltd, 80 Strand, London WC2R 0RL, England
Penguin Group (USA) Inc., 375 Hudson Street, New York, New York 10014, USA
Penguin Group (Australia) Ltd, 250 Camberwell Road, Camberwell, Victoria, 3124, Australia
(a division of Pearson Australia Group Pty Ltd)
Canada, India, New Zealand, South Africa

Published by BBC Children's Books, 2006

10 9 8 7 6 5 4 3 2 1

ISBN 978 1 405 90321 9

Printed in the United Kingdom

ROBIN HOOD

PARENT HOOD

Adapted by Mandy Archer from the television
script "Parent Hood" by Dominic Minghella
for the television series Robin Hood created
by Dominic Minghella and Foz Allan for
Tiger Aspect as shown on BBC One.

CHAPTER ONE

Robin of Locksley expertly brought the Sheriff's horse to a standstill and dismounted. He grinned broadly at the band of men gathered round him in the forest clearing.

'Definitely one of your better ideas Roy,' he complimented.

Roy, one of the youngest outlaws in the group, slid off his horse and grasped Robin's fist in celebration.

'Do we like it?' he smirked.

'I think we do!' laughed Robin, as he engaged in an elaborate handshake. The ritual was well-rehearsed, just one small gesture between men that lived and breathed as brothers.

Roy's plot to steal the horses from under the nose of Nottingham's Master At Arms, Guy of Gisborne, had come off like a dream. Luring Gisborne's horsemen into the forest had almost been too easy. Robin was the perfect decoy; just one jibe had sent Gisborne and his men plunging into the forest after him. The riders had reached full gallop by the time Robin had hurtled towards the tripwire where Roy, Will, Allan and Much were hiding. The Sheriff's men were thrown to the ground in quick succession, leaving Robin and his friends to ride off into the sunset.

'Well done mate.'

It was Allan's turn to shake hands with Roy. Their morning's work was guaranteed to infuriate Gisborne, but for Allan that just made it taste all the sweeter. His motives for turning his back on Nottingham society were not as honourable as Robin's, but he shared a healthy loathing for the Sheriff's rotten regime.

'Whoa, there!'

Much's horse spooked as he struggled to tether it to an oak tree. Robin's loyal manservant eventually flopped to the ground then scrambled over to join in the camaraderie. Roy reached out his hand to Much and started the familiar routine, before pulling it sharply away at the last moment.

'Oh very funny,' said Much. The snub hurt. After five years of desperate fighting side-by-side against the Turks, he was still getting over the disappointment of not returning to see his master resume his position rightful place as Lord of Locksley. Robin had ruled

that option out very quickly – from the moment he witnessed the cruel poverty and impossible taxes that had been imposed upon his village. Opposing the corrupt new Sheriff meant death, so Robin had dragged Much kicking and screaming into the shadows of Sherwood Forest. They had fallen in with an unlikely band of fellow outlaws, a clan of "dead" men each with their own reason for dropping out of society. Much admired Robin's own vow to help the poor get through these dark days, but it didn't mean he had to like it. He watched Roy laughing at him and frowned. Some of his new bedfellows were no more than rascals and thieves.

A small whimper echoed round the clearing.

'Much,' sighed Robin. 'Don't be so easily wounded.'

Roy wasn't so bothered. 'As it was my idea, I get to keep the nag, right?'

Much scowled and turned his back on the group. *Typical.*

'Nag? This is a fine pedigree war horse!' Robin smiled, then nodded. 'It's yours. Well-deserved my friend.'

There was another whimper from Much's direction. The men exchanged tired looks and groaned silently.

Roy petulantly held out the stallion's reins. 'You have it, if you're going to cry about it.'

Much whisked round at once, bringing himself up to his full height. Unfortunately it was only enough to reach Roy's chin. 'I am not crying!'

'Much…' Before Robin could step in, he was interrupted by a full-blown shriek. The cry was followed by another and another in alarming succession. The men wordlessly tracked the sound, silently beating a path through the forest undergrowth. Suddenly Robin stopped near a bank of rabbit holes and pulled back some ferns. A scarlet-faced baby lay nestled in the leaves, screaming with all its might. Will nervously crouched down to pick it up.

'What is it?' Much was completely thrown. 'I mean I know what it is, but…'

'It's a boy,' said Will.

Allan whistled and shook his head. 'We rode straight through here. We could have trampled it.'

Will wrapped the newborn's velvet shawl round it more tightly. 'This baby is cold. Its mother is long gone.'

Roy winced. 'Can't you stop it crying?'

'Here.' Allan stepped forward and grabbed the

child by its ankles, dangling it upside down in one deft movement.

The spectators all gasped.

Allan eyed them defensively. 'What? That's how you shut them up.'

The baby opened its mouth and after a moment of horrible silence, belted out a strangulated cry. Robin seized the bundle and cradled it in his arms.

Roy clapped his hands together and got ready to move off. 'Right! Leave it here then. Let's go.'

Much was horrified. 'You cannot leave a baby.'

'What do you want to do with it? We're outlaws, not wet nurses.'

Suddenly the forest was still again. The baby was silently gazing up at Robin, grasping his thumb with its tiny hand.

'How do you do that?' asked Will.

Robin smirked proudly. 'He likes me.'

It was time to leave while they could. Robin led the way out of the thicket, carefully shielding the baby under his leather jerkin.

As they picked their way back to the clearing, Allan marvelled at the pock-marked earth. 'It's a miracle that baby's alive. There are hoof prints everywhere, look.'

Robin glanced down, then froze. Something about those hoof prints made his blood run cold.

He whispered to the others. 'No movement. No noise.'

The outlaws were absolutely still – they knew from experience that their lives might depend on it. Robin listened to all the sounds of the forest, then relaxed a touch.

'Look at these hoof prints,' he beckoned to Much. 'They are marked. Gisborne is not the idiot he looks. He will track us.'

The men looked suspiciously over their shoulders, carefully taking this new threat on board.

Much smugly turned back to Roy. 'You didn't think of that, did you?'

Roy refused to catch Much's eye. He'd been out-manoeuvred by Gisborne and everyone knew it.

This time Allan broke up the tiff. 'Not being funny, but shouldn't we be moving on? They could be coming already.'

Robin nodded and made a cautious move towards the horses. A move too late.

'They could be *here* already,' announced a satisfied voice.

With a confident click, a black horse was spurred forward from the shadows. Guy of Gisborne looked down at Robin from his mount, beaming from ear-to-ear.

CHAPTER TWO

'M aster!' cried Much. 'What do we do?'
He squinted up at Gisborne then
gradually took in the throng of dark figures stepping
out of the trees. Much could feel his heart pounding
beneath his shirt. The outlaws were totally surrounded
by the Sheriff's soldiers. Some were on horseback,
some were on foot, but all had their swords drawn
and ready.

'What can we do?' shrugged Robin. 'We do not
believe in needlessly harming man or beast.' He
sighed then rocked the baby, not taking his eyes off
Gisborne for a second.

Much was totally flummoxed. 'What?!'

'Vermin, on the other hand is a totally different
matter.'

Robin broke into a board grin and drew his sword.
Tucking the baby under his left arm, he charged
straight towards the Sheriff's men.

Within seconds, outlaw and soldier were blurred
in a frenzy of hand-to-hand fighting. Robin's

men couldn't match the costly steel weaponry of Gisborne's troop, but they had the ingenuity to tie them up in knots.

Allan took his longbow and wielded it like a sabre at a soldier carrying a heavy broadsword. His opponent scoffed at the match. His broadsword flashed and gleamed in the sunlight – a true killing machine against the flimsy wood of a longbow.

Before facing the inevitable blow, Allan suddenly darted forward and poked the longbow in the soldier's eyes. 'Gotcha!'

The Sheriff's man buckled in half, clutching his bloody face.

'Aaagggh!' Much surged forward belting out his usual war cry, a strangulated blend of rage and terror. His first victim was awarded a mighty blow to the helmet. Much whooped with delight then moved on as the soldier sank giddily to the forest floor.

While Will wrenched a horseman out of his saddle, Roy was engaged in a fierce one-on-one skirmish in the undergrowth. Still smarting from Gisborne's trick, his eyes were fired with rage. When his opponent tripped on a thick root, Roy spotted his advantage. He grabbed the soldier's arm and twisted it behind his back, before sinking his teeth into the man's ear.

As Roy's man flailed past him, another Sheriff's man struck Robin on the side of the head.

'Do you mind? I was just getting the baby to sleep.' Robin was thoroughly enjoying himself, he liked nothing better than the adrenaline rush of combat. Fighting with a baby in one arm was starting to be a serious handicap however, and his opponent was coming in for more.

Robin neatly side-stepped the charging soldier, somehow managing to deliver a strike to the man's head on the way. The soldier fell heavily backwards, taking Robin's sword with him. Robin smiled happily and allowed himself a moment to comfort the baby.

'All right, little one?'

Will glanced over his shoulder at Robin, then widened his eyes in panic. Behind him a heavy-set man was preparing to sink his broadsword into the back of Robin's head.

'Robin!' cried Will.

Robin turned just in time, but he was totally defenceless.

'Catch!'

Will gasped as Robin threw the baby to his adversary, banking on the man's gut reaction.

Robin's judgement was shrewd. Confused, the Sheriff's man dropped his metal and opened his arms to catch the infant. Will saw his chance and knocked the man out with a solid crack on the head. As the man crumpled to the ground, the baby began to cry.

'Now look,' scolded Robin. 'We're going to have to start all over again.' He gently lifted the baby out of the falling man's arms, letting his opponent's body thud heavily back on the mud. He chuckled happily, confident that the outlaws were winning this particular fight.

From his position on the sidelines, Gisborne was growing more and more irritated. He spurred his horse into the fray then sneered at his men.

'Idiots. Get up!'

It was a fiasco. Seeing his calls were useless, Gisborne picked up his mace and circled it furiously round and round his head.

'Try this!'

The studded mace was sent tearing through the air, straight on course for his prime target – Robin Hood. Anticipating the impact, Roy dived towards Robin, pushing both him and the baby onto the ground. Robin rolled over as gently as he could,

protecting the babe in his arms, but the mace caught Roy on its trajectory. Roy screamed in pain then fell.

While Gisborne's men hurriedly re-saddled, two soldiers grabbed Roy and dragged him to the clearing. In a gruff flurry of shouting and horse hooves Gisborne and his men were gone, taking Roy with them.

'Robin!'

Robin winced as his friend's desperate cry echoed through the forest, but it was too late to save him.

'They got Roy,' stuttered Much, somehow trying to fill the void left by his absence. 'Sorry.'

Robin didn't answer. There was nothing to say.

Sensing the mood change, the baby suddenly started to cry. The unrelenting wails crescendoed, snapping Robin back to the here and now.

'Shut that thing up.'

Back at the camp, Little John was starting to feel uneasy. Roy's plan was taking too long. The instant he glimpsed the silhouettes of the horseless men flicking through the trees, he knew something was drastically wrong. He crouched over the fire he had been building and waited for the bombshell.

'John…' began Robin, grappling for the right words.

'They got Roy,' said Allan at once.

John stood up, his head reeling. He'd been an outlaw for several years now and the lad had become like a son to him. It was Roy who had helped John adapt to his life as a 'dead man', living rough in the forest, away from his wife. He had given John comfort and companionship.

'They tracked us. The horses were marked,' Much tried to explain, but Little John was now looking aghast at the baby in Robin's arms. 'Oh… it's a baby.'

John flashed Much a withering look. That was obvious.

Much kept on talking. 'No, I was just saying…'

Little John turned his back on him. He could feel the blood boiling up to the surface and his fingers tingled with rage. Roy was gone and it was a struggle to keep control.

'John,' said Robin quietly. 'I am sorry.'

Little John kicked out the campfire and looked each man in the eye.

'We go to Nottingham.'

'My name is Royston White. I fight for Robin Hood and King Richard.'

Roy's throat was dry, but he forced himself to utter the mantra he'd been taught to say under capture.

Gisborne's simple answer was to batter Roy with a brutal punch across the jaw. Roy staggered onto the dungeon floor, while Gisborne prepared to hit him again.

'It would be wise, would it not, to break his jaw after he has talked, rather than before?' mused the Sheriff of Nottingham, stepping into the dismal cell. 'Who is he?'

Gisborne roughly tore Roy's dog tag from his neck then pulled himself up straight. 'One of Locksley's associates. Raided my stables. Unfortunately for them, I have had all my horses shod with an identifying mark, which allowed me to track…'

The Sheriff silenced his Man At Arms with a disinterested wave of the hand. He carefully lifted his black robe and stepped forward to study Roy from head to foot.

'Talk.'

Roy focussed his eyes on the dank ceiling and repeated the words he'd learnt. He clenched his muscles and braced himself for the torrent of physical abuse to come.

'I'll say no more.'

'You've said enough. It must have been a difficult day for you.' The Sheriff's response was gentle, almost soothing.

'What?' Roy was frightened now. Why wasn't he being tortured, kicked, at least sworn at?

Gisborne shot a look of irritation at the Sheriff, but his master was the picture of compassion.

'We let our friend rest.'

'What is happening here?' asked Roy.

The Sheriff put his finger up to his lips and smiled graciously, ushering Gisborne out of the cell.

As the heavy door creaked back into its setting, Gisborne urged his case.

'He will not talk, I can assure you, unless he is beaten.'

The Sheriff nodded appreciatively, but stopped his aide from going any further.

'First see if he has any relatives in Nottingham.'

CHAPTER THREE

'Canon Richard,' announced a castle steward, as Nottingham's most senior priest glided into the room. He, like all the other lords and aristocrats standing in the grand hall, held an esteemed place on the Council of Nobles.

A servant unfastened Lord Loughborough's wool cloak and ushered him towards the ancient oak table. He had been riding since dawn to get to this Council session, but coughed anxiously when he noticed that he was the last to enter the chamber. Since King Richard had been away, the Council's law-making powers had been recalled in all but name by the incoming Sheriff. Sheriff Vaizey ruled with an iron fist, unable to tolerate resistance at any level.

Loughborough smiled weakly when he caught the eye of his friend, Lord Woodvale. Although both men knew that their role on the Council was a mere formality, non-attendance was out of the question. The Sheriff used these Council sessions to implement his latest schemes and to grill each man on the amount of tax collected on their estates.

When she could see that the Sheriff had been made comfortable, Marian drew back a carved oak chair and gently guided her father to his seat. As the old sheriff, Sir Edward still commanded some respect in Nottingham, even if his ability to influence this dark new era was pitiable.

Marian was careful to set her own place a discreet distance back from the table. Only permitted at the meeting in her capacity as Sir Edward's nursemaid, she was not even entitled to speak.

When the Sheriff cleared his throat it was barely audible, but somehow the gentle discourse amongst the lords hushed immediately.

'News from the village of Clun is good. No new cases for a fortnight,' the Sheriff announced. 'The pestilence, whatever it was, is gone.'

Sir Edward sighed with relief. 'Then we can lift the quarantine. Feed the survivors.'

Marian looked to the Sheriff for confirmation, but he was clearly not in the mood.

'The people of Clun are grubby people. The great unwashed. Low on taxes and high on moaning.' He stared idly at a fingernail, rotating his hand in the light, then shook his head. 'The quarantine remains.'

'They must be fed!' declared Marian. 'They will die!'

Blood flooded to her cheeks, as she felt every man in the room turn his eyes toward her. She should never have spoken, it was a silly mistake. Marian despised everything about the Sheriff, but she could never let anyone in his court suspect this for an instant. Opposing the Sheriff meant death – it didn't scare her, but she knew she could do more as an aristocratic lady than she could ever do as a marked fugitive. She envied Robin Hood and his band of men in many ways, but she was intelligent enough to realise that her position had its uses. Marian was privy to most of the Sheriff's new schemes and was free to draw on all her resources to undermine them from the inside.

'Marian…'

Sir Edward shot his daughter a pleading look, but the Sheriff smiled generously. Marian checked herself and respectfully lowered her head, allowing her tumbling dark hair to cover her flashing eyes.

'My dear, you have to understand. These are incapable people. They do not help themselves. We cannot and must not nanny them.'

Marian turned her head to the top of the table.

'But how can they help themselves if we do not allow them to leave their village?'

The Sheriff nodded patiently. 'I agree. It is a conundrum.'

Inexplicably the Sheriff yawned, then paused to sip some wine from his goblet.

'Another conundrum is this – whom would we tax to pay for food for the hopeless people of Clun?' The Sheriff now turned his attention to the rest of the Council. 'Would you have me rob Peter to pay Paul?'

The company just about managed to bolster the Sheriff with a weak array of nods and approving mumbles.

'Simpler to leave the quarantine in place. Then, in a week or two, we announce that the village has been,' the Sheriff paused to select the right word, '*cleansed.*'

Marian watched the Nobles brace themselves. It was cold-blooded murder, but none of them were even prepared to look the perpetrator in the eye. She watched Lord Woodvale take a moment to recover his composure and slowly nod in agreement. His cowardice was infuriating, but understandable.

The Sheriff delicately ran his finger around

the top of his goblet then sank back into the ornate chair.

'I may house a garrison there.'

The real agenda was emerging at last.

'We cannot let healthy people die!' Marian's voice again echoed around the panelled chamber. Edward tensed and put his arm on her sleeve, but this time she had leapt to her feet.

'This is barbaric! If it became known…' Marian's voice tapered off. She immediately cursed herself for raising such a direct challenge.

'Interesting,' mused the Sheriff, still smiling. 'Fire in the belly. Is this reason talking? Or is it frustration? Frustration at being – how old? – and still a maiden?'

The nobles sniggered gratefully at the opportunity to disassociate themselves from the girl. Marian coloured and returned to her seat. Under the table she wordlessly sank her fingernails into her palms. She felt physically sick.

Sir Edward met his daughter's eyes and frowned. Neither of them could afford for her role as nursemaid to be questioned. In her public life, any political viewpoint or signs of intelligence had to be squashed in favour of tapestry and pressed flowers. It was a difficult role for Marian to play convincingly, but both their lives depended on it.

A servant came up and whispered discreetly in the Sheriff's ear.

'Excuse me. I have other business.'

The Council rose in unison as the Sheriff was helped out of his chair. He turned and bowed graciously to his inner circle, then directed a generous smile towards Marian and her father. It was only when he'd reached the sanctuary of the castle corridor that he allowed himself to grimace.

CHAPTER FOUR

Annie scuttled past the burning torch illuminating the dim stone corridor, carrying an unappealing woven basket loaded with hard hunks of stale bread.

'Guy?'

The Master At Arms was stalking towards her at some speed, his leather greatcoat trailing behind him.

'What?' His response was irritated, self-conscious.

The serving girl looked over her shoulder, then lowered her voice to a whisper. 'You are back quickly…?'

Gisborne paused for an instant before grunting his agreement.

'Did he cry?' Her words seemed too haunted, too desperate for such a young woman.

Roy watched from the hatch in his cell door as Gisborne turned on his heels and marched away without giving an answer. Annie gazed longingly at his disappearing shadow, then pushed Roy's excuse for a meal through the hatch.

'How can you smile at him?' Roy had to ask.

Annie spoke softly. 'He has another side. A side he cannot show.'

'You are wrong.'

Annie shook her head. 'Be careful. If I had position, I would be his wife.'

Roy chuckled sourly. 'He tells you that, does he?'

'I am the mother of his child,' said Annie coldly.

Roy turned his swollen, bruised face up to the light, then moved nearer to the hatch so the girl could see him.

'Look what he did to me. Keep your child away from him.'

'Shut up!' cried Annie, recklessly raising her voice. 'He is a good man. He has found a home for my baby at the Abbey of Kirklees. This is not cheap. It will cost money.'

Annie snatched the rotten bread out of Roy's fist, then tore back to the kitchens, hot tears streaming down her face.

Roy cursed and then abruptly sat down between the foul puddles on the dungeon floor. *Two babies in one day – now wouldn't that be a coincidence?*

'What is he called, your baby?' asked Roy at supper.

Annie wanted to ignore the prisoner, but his question compelled her to stop.

'None of your business,' she answered, then, 'Seth.' It was a relief just to say his name.

Roy sniffed, then concentrated on breaking up the bread.

'He's a few weeks old. Dark hair, lots of it.'

Annie looked up immediately.

'He also has a velvet shawl?' Roy could see he was making the connection.

'Yes. Did you meet him on the way to the Abbey?'

Annie peered through the bars, searching Roy's eyes.

Roy gave up on the bread, opening his hand to let the crumbs drop down near a rat scuttling across the foul stone floor.

'Sort of.'

Annie caught her breath, trying to draw some meaning from this. In the silence, Roy stared past the girl at the ominous black shape looming up behind her. The happy father had arrived.

Gisborne pointed at Roy. 'Sheriff wants to

see you.'

'I'll be blunt. I have a favour to ask.'

The Sheriff's opulent study reeked of wealth, ancestry and status, yet his face was impish, full of mischief.

Roy locked his jaw and focussed on the ornate candlestick burning in the window.

'So sullen?' The Sheriff's smirk widened as he reached for a small scarlet pouch that had been resting amongst the scrolls and papers on his desk. Slowly and thoughtfully, the Sheriff drew a brilliant dagger from the pouch, turning it over and over in the light.

'I'd be very grateful if you would use this on our mutual friend Robin Hood.'

The Sheriff paused for a response, but Roy wasn't giving him the pleasure just yet. 'Bring me his head on a plate. Or no plate. I have plenty of plates.'

Gisborne laughed quietly, but Roy's response was sober.

'I'd sooner kill my own mother.'

The Sheriff clapped his hands in delight then nodded to Gisborne. 'What an amazing coincidence!'

As the Man At Arms stepped out of the room, the

Sheriff sprang out of his chair and approached Roy.

'Of course when people say things like "I'd sooner kill my own mother", they rarely have such a statement tested.' The Sheriff was leaning forward to whisper in his captive's ear, invading his personal space to such a degree that Roy almost toppled backwards. As the door creaked back open, Roy felt the hairs rise on the back of his neck.

Gisborne was jabbing his glove into the back of a frail and terrified woman, forcing her into the light.

'Mother...'

'Royston? But you're...' Mary White stumbled backwards towards a guard, giddy with shock. She hadn't seen her son for two awful years, since he had been hanged at Loughborough. *How could he be standing here?*

'I was going to come back. When things were better. But they were never better.'

His mother nodded and struggled to her feet again, as if she almost understood. As if the last two years of grieving might actually have just been a terrible dream.

'The baskets. The presents of food and money – was that you?'

Roy felt as if his heart was about to be ripped

from his chest.

As his guards fought to restrain the outlaw, the Sheriff absorbed the scene like a little boy in a sweet shop. He sucked his finger thoughtfully, toying with his next move.

'I like this. This is good, isn't it?' The Sheriff held out both his hands, weighing one up against the other. 'The horns of a dilemma – kill Robin, kill mother. Which is it to be?'

The Sheriff's black eyes darted between the mother and son, but he was forced to crane his neck to catch Roy's answer.

'I will not do it.'

The Sheriff paused. This was proving to be a marvellous challenge. 'I don't think you understand what a dilemma means. It means you have to do one or the other. You have to decide.'

Silence filled the room.

This time the Sheriff spoke slowly and deliberately, as if training a disobedient child. 'And if you do not, let's just say that I'll decide for you.'

The Sheriff carefully offered the dagger to Roy one more time.

Roy pinched his eyes together in concentration, but his mother's weeping was thundering round and

round his head. His hand was shaking as he snatched the assassin's blade.

Gisborne and the Sheriff exchanged satisfied smiles.

'Shall we say by sunrise tomorrow? I don't know about you, but I work best to a deadline.' Somehow the Sheriff managed to completely ignore the old woman's cries for mercy, even though they were escalating into desperate shrieks. Suddenly he erupted into spontaneous laughter. 'Of course when people say 'deadline', they do not usually mean that someone will be dead at the end of it!'

CHAPTER FIVE

'**I**'ll give him one more minute then we're out of here!' Little John almost spat the words out under his breath. The big, hulking man was crouched on all fours amongst the unforgiving branches of a sloe tree – he had thorns pushing their way under his vest and Will Scarlett leaning his full weight against one elbow.

'Shhhh…' Robin pleaded with his eyes and put a finger up to John's lips. Their hiding place in the brush at the edge of Sherwood Forest was vulnerable in the extreme. He shared Little John's desperation to get to Roy, but this matter had to be sorted first.

Suddenly the sound of heavy boots thundered towards them. As he staggered towards the men Much was red-faced and speechless with exhaustion, but the bawling baby made enough noise for the entire company.

Little John shook his head and raised himself to his full height, knocking Will to the floor on the way. Not much point hiding after that racket.

'Sorry,' stuttered Much. 'Nobody wants another mouth to feed.'

Robin frowned. 'You told them that I would provide for the child?'

'Yes, but to be honest I think that the noise thing…' Much whispered, shielding the infant as he wiped his nose on his sleeve. 'It won't shut up. And its head is loose. Do you think that's right?'

Robin reached for the baby, still frowning at the rejection.

'I'll go down and ask,' said Will. 'Give it to me.'

Little John violently thrust his staff into the sloe tree. 'There's no time.'

Robin wasn't sure what to do about it, but one thing was patently obvious – they weren't going to be able to go anywhere unless this wretched child stopped crying. He awkwardly shifted the straps from his quiver and cradled the baby into his chest.

'WAHH!'

Robin's nurturing arms made no difference whatsoever. Acknowledging Little John's scowl, he instinctively turned and paced away from the forest boundary. His rhythmic footfall hushed the baby almost at once.

'Where are you going?' It was Allan A Dale, back

from a scouting mission at the castle.

Robin looked at the man as if he was an imbecile. 'I am walking. If I stop walking the baby cries.' Robin loitered on the spot for a moment, wincing at the wail that emerged straight afterwards. 'See?'

Allan raised his eyes then reeled off his findings. 'Central courtyard. The portcullis. All heavily manned.'

Robin paced deeper into the forest, forcing his men to trail after him. 'The east wall, where the builders are working?'

'Teeming.'

'How about the south wall?' asked Will.

'No, it's too high,' said Robin, getting into his stride.

The men were now walking five-abreast, every one in step until Allan stopped in his tracks. 'Not being funny or anything, but is this a great idea?'

Little John growled.

'Roy is my son.'

Much couldn't resist opening his mouth. 'He is not actually your son.'

'Like a son.' His voice was not much more than a rasp.

'Say like a son, then.' Much didn't often get the

chance to pull anyone else up on anything. 'Don't say he is your son. It's confusing.'

As usual, the other men completely ignored him.

Allan felt it was time for a reality check. 'Even if we got in, I heard the new door to the dungeons is two foot thick.'

'You…' Little John swung for Allan, a huge haymaker of a punch that Robin just managed to block with his free arm.

'John, no.'

'I heard that too about the door,' added Will.

Robin looked back at John and understood his exasperation. No matter what the odds, they had to get into that castle.

Will continued. 'But I also heard Robert of York put it in.'

'And?'

Will's face broke into an infectious grin. 'He can't make a hinge to save his life. The lock side will be as strong as an ox. The *hinge* side will be weak. Especially with the weight of two foot of timber.'

Robin instantly started to plot it out in his mind. 'Much?'

His manservant stepped forward, pleased to sanction the theory. 'I am sure Will is right.'

'No.' Robin handed him the baby back. 'I cannot think and walk.'

'What me?' Much was horrified. 'Again…?'

Robin wasn't listening. He picked a forked stick off the forest floor then began to draw in the mud. 'So the door is breachable. If we can get over the wall in the first place, taking this southern approach.'

Robin's voice was drowned by the renewed round of screeches from the baby in Much's arms. At last his position was vindicated. 'See? I'm walking but he cries.'

Robin sighed then carried on sketching.

'On no, Master!'

The men turned to see Much holding the child out at arm's length, his face contorted with absolute revulsion. 'We need a woman, quick!'

'Why did it have to be my sleeve?'

Will deftly tucked in the baby's new nappy, chuckling at Much all the while. It had been a smelly business, but it was definitely worth it if only to enjoy the panicked expression on Much's face. Besides, his cuff had been just the thing for the job.

Much nursed his exposed wrist, about to repeat his protest until he met Little John's eye.

'We rescue Roy. Now.'

Allan held back. 'What is the point of us all dying?'

His concept of honour was more than a little battered round the edges. Living amongst exiles suited him, but who had decided they should become family? Besides, every one of them secretly knew the plan was ropy to say the least.

'"For every man there is a purpose which he sets up in his life. Let yours be the doing of all good deeds."' Robin shrugged. 'That's us, lads.'

'That the Bible?' asked Will.

'It's the Qu'ran.'

'The what?'

Much explained. 'It's the Turk Bible. He read it out in the Holy Land.'

'Why?' Allan was mystified.

Robin gently rested the baby over his shoulder and started to saddle up. 'I wanted to know what it was that we were fighting.'

'What are you going to do with that?' Allan gestured up to the sleeping baby.

'It cannot be left.'

Allan laughed incredulously, tightening up his horse's girth. 'It cannot come either. What are you

going to do, give him a little bow and quiver?'

But Robin had already mounted, strapping the baby against his chest.

Roy's horse was also saddled and ready. The Sheriff's men had unlocked the heavy castle gates, leaving their prisoner to stand unchained in the middle of the courtyard. Roy was frozen to the spot, caught in a terrible tension between fight or flight. The Sheriff circled his prey for a few agonising minutes, then impulsively lurched forward and tore at his shirt.

'You have made a heroic escape I think, don't you?' The Sheriff turned to the six chain-mailed men, mounting up behind them. 'My men are determined to catch you.'

Roy had nothing to say. Irritated at his composure, the Sheriff tied Roy's dog tag back round his neck.

'Don't forget your little badge of honour.'

Roy instinctively reached up to touch the talisman, remembering how Will had carved one for each of Robin's men. This was the first time he had been separated from the tag and now he could almost feel it burning into his chest.

The Sheriff snapped his fingers. 'Well go on then, run!'

Roy threw himself onto the Sheriff's mount, digging his heels into its flank.

'Yahh!' Roy's horse thundered out of the courtyard, galloping towards the toll gates at a blistering pace. Beneath the deafening thud of hooves, he could hear the Sheriff's men spur themselves into pursuit. Roy leant forward in the saddle and gripped onto the horse's waxy mane. If only he could just gallop on and on, forever.

'Roy!'

Suddenly Little John was there, riding alongside him. The rest of the band were just behind, their horses' teeth flashing as they pushed them forward at an impossible pace. Roy gasped with guilt when he realised that his friends had been outside the castle gates, waiting, planning a rescue.

'This way!' It was Robin – vigilant as always he'd quickly sized up the Sheriff's sergeants emerging out of the horizon.

Little John reached over and grabbed Roy's reins, masterfully bringing the horse round in the opposite direction. Roy looked over his shoulder, then spurred the mare forward into the sanctuary of Sherwood Forest.

CHAPTER SIX

'Stop here.'

Robin's men disappeared into a copse of ancient horse chestnut trees; hooves thudding across the thick roots that poked out of the mud. As soon as they came to a halt, Roy slid off his mare and started to loosen its tack. The animal was dripping with sweat, its legs caked with earth thrown up by the gallop.

Robin grinned as he unbuckled the straps that tied the baby to him. The Sheriff's sergeants had been lost some three miles' back, stranded by a stream at the edge of the Forest. He looked over at Roy, satisfied to have brought him back where he belonged. Everyone was enjoying the high, but it was a full minute before any man had the energy to speak.

'Roy.' Little John broke the silence, holding out his arms to embrace the boy.

Roy nodded and smiled weakly, then sidestepped John to get round to the other side of his horse.

CHAPTER SIX

The older man looked confused, but decided to bite his tongue.

'It's good to have you back!' Robin gave Roy a hearty slap on the back, not noticing how his friend jumped at the touch. Inside Roy was like a coiled spring, but he fought quickly to compose himself.

'Good to *be* back,' he nodded.

Allan rubbed his hands together in anticipation, ready for the gory details. 'How'd you escape?'

'Oh you know, showed the Sheriff some of my moves!' Roy played out a pantomime fighting sequence, he knew they'd love this. 'Reckon he was impressed. Reckon he was going to ask me to join his side.'

The men laughed heartily and savoured the victory. As they each grasped Roy's hand and hugged, only Much was frowning. Moments like this made him long for the days when it was just him and Robin – he couldn't stomach all this bravado. He had hoped Roy's party piece might get cut short when the baby started to whimper, but Robin simply handed the child over to Much before turning back to the returning hero.

'*Moves*. What does that mean?' Much muttered under his breath. As the baby appeared to be the

51

only one prepared to listen, he decided to talk to him.

Roy rested against a tree trunk, entertaining his court. 'But I said to him, no thanks mate, I don't do red wine from Burgundy. I'm an October Ale man, me.'

Little John laughed and watched him proudly, his weathered hands whittling a twig with a blade from his pocket.

'How many did you take down?' Allan wanted the body count.

Roy closed his eyes for a moment, hesitating as he tried to get his story straight.

'Stop! Stop! He's going to kill us!'

It was Much, suddenly shouting at the top of his voice.

'What?' Roy didn't know what to do.

'Who?' asked Allan.

Much pointed at Roy, eyes wide as dinner plates.

'Much?' Robin braced his servant with both arms, trying to calm him down.

'The horse... the horse... the same trick,' Much was struggling to get the words out. 'He's led them right to us. We are done for.'

The men leapt to their feet, but Robin was there

already. He quickly approached the spot where the Sheriff's horse was grazing and lifted each of the hooves. Relaxing, he turned a foot towards them to show the shoes were unmarked.

'Much!' Will's relief spilled out as frustration.

Much coloured with embarrassment. 'It was possible, you have to admit.'

The men shook their heads, then gradually drifted apart to rest. The air of celebration had evaporated – although Much was wrong this time they all knew that he could have so easily been right.

Roy seized his chance to get Robin alone.

'Robin, I have something to tell you.'

'What?'

Roy gestured towards the company, guiding Robin to the shadows behind a gnarled horse chestnut. He felt the dagger glinting inside his breast pocket and took a deep breath.

'I have something…'

Robin looked him straight in the eye. 'Roy?'

Roy paused and summoned all his strength to return Robin's stare. Silently he slid his hand into his waistcoat, fixing his hand around the knife. It was a subtle, fine movement, but Robin sensed it.

'What?'

Suddenly Roy took his hand off the dagger. Will strolled up to the men, whistling as he snapped off pieces of kindling to pack in the horses' saddlebags. The moment was broken, but Robin's face was still clouded with suspicion.

'I know the baby's name.' Roy was busking it the best he could.

'Our baby?' Robin was thrown.

Seeing that the trust was still there, Roy found the strength to recover himself. 'It's Seth.'

'Seth?' Will and Robin were both captivated.

'I met his father, in the castle dungeon. Stealing bread. Looks like the mother. She must have panicked at the thought of raising the child alone and taken it out to the woods.'

Roy's eyes darted between the two men. *If only it was true.*

'This Sheriff,' Will was furious, 'he's destroying lives.'

Roy fixed his attention on Robin. 'The mother lives in Knighton. You and I should take him home. Give her some money to keep the child.'

Robin was still thinking when Much approached. He'd roughly tucked the baby under his buckskin shirt to keep warm, leaving the child to peer out the

best it could past the folds of his cloak.

'Can we move on?' asked Much.

Robin eyed the child then raised his voice to address the whole company. 'Meet at the Long Stone at sunset.'

'Where are you going?'

'To Knighton. To take the baby home.' Robin patted Roy on the shoulder. 'Roy knows where he lives.'

Much nodded eagerly. 'I'll come.'

'No!' Roy struggled to calm his voice. 'More than two, and we attract attention.'

'Yes, of course.' Much sighed. 'I'll sort things out here. I thought we could have rabbit, rabbit for supper. What do you…?'

His voice trailed off. Much climbed on a fallen tree to get a proper look, but Robin and Roy had already disappeared into the shadows of the Forest with the baby.

CHAPTER SEVEN

'Lady Marian.' The young sergeant bowed in deference to the noblewoman in front of him then pulled himself up to his full height. He and his officers had been guarding the barricaded village of Clun for weeks now, but he had never expected a visit from such a distinguished member of the Sheriff's circle.

'Good day,' Marian looked down from the buggy of her cart. 'It is... Peter, isn't it?'

'Yes.' The man was surprised, astonished that she could actually know of him.

Marian greeted the sergeant with a warm smile. 'Peter, I have heard good things about you from my Lord the Sheriff.'

'What kind of things?' Peter removed his helmet and stepped forward.

'You are a hardworking, intelligent man, well-placed for promotion I believe...' Marian edged her horse on a touch, nodding to the battery of soldiers picketing the wattle fence that circled the village.

Peter was flattered. 'Really? I hardly think…' but as he squinted up at Marian, something made him stop. *Why was a lady of such standing travelling alone in a tradesman's cart?*

'What do you want?' His voice was cool now, suspicious.

Marian leant down and whispered gently, using her big blue eyes to their optimum effect. 'I need five minutes in the village.'

Peter clamped his helmet over his chain mail and stepped back again. 'That I cannot do.'

'Please.'

'I cannot. *Did she think he was stupid?*

Marian could see she was getting nowhere. It was time to sharpen her tone. 'Step aside, I have business in this village.'

She clicked her tongue authoritatively to drive the cart forward, but Peter quickly reached for the horse's bridle. 'There is a quarantine, surely you know that. Pestilence.'

Marian's voice was scathing. 'The pestilence is long gone, you know that, and if you don't you are a fool.'

The rest of the soldiers were taking an interest now, surrounding the cart and tugging curiously at

the hemp cloth pulled taut over its contents.

'The Sheriff's orders. I cannot let you in.'

'I am the daughter of the old Sheriff, and *I* am ordering you to stand aside. The people in here are starving.'

One of the soldiers ripped the cloth with his knife, tearing the sheet back to reveal rows of baskets packed underneath.

As he watched Marian turn in her seat, Peter could see that she was almost quivering with rage. He grinned, now it was his turn to be the one in power.

'If the Sheriff knew your game, he'd have your guts for garters. I'm right, aren't I?'

The sergeant darted forward and flipped a basket open. It was crammed with meat pies, his favourite. He whisked a pie out, just eluding Marian's desperate lunge to swipe it back. He sunk his teeth in and started to eat.

Marian dropped the reins and stood up to shout at to the jeering men. 'The pestilence is gone. These people need food.'

Peter took another bite, then tossed the pie on the floor. 'Nice pie, how about a nice kiss to go with it?'

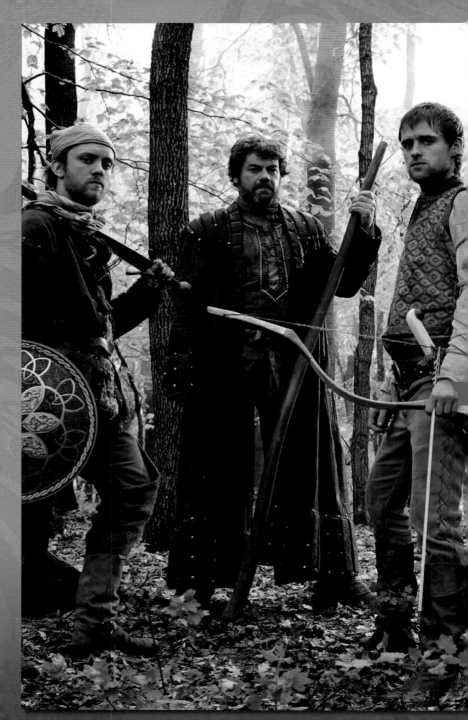

It was hopeless. Marian moved to circle her horse, but Peter caught her arm.

'Don't you touch me!' White with anger, she pulled a short sword out of her cloak and flashed it up against Peter's neck.

Oblivious to their sergeant's predicament, the Sheriff's soldiers descended like vultures on the cart, snatching at the loaves, meat and eggs that Marian had struggled so hard to buy. Marian bit her lip with frustration. If she had been in disguise, she would not have stood for this; she would have fought back. However, as herself, Marian knew it would be foolish to make a scene.

One of the men waved jovially in response to Marian's glare and raised a particularly plump pie to his lips.

It never made it.

An arrow came out of nowhere, spearing the pie and knocking it onto the floor. The men froze.

'Everybody still if you please.'

Robin's horse was standing just a few yards away, Roy next to him with his bow drawn and ready. He bowed courteously to Marian.

'Having a little trouble?' Robin's face was a picture of charm.

'It is nothing I cannot resolve myself thank you,' said Marian. She was grateful for Robin's help, but it was extremely galling that it was he who had come to her rescue. He was such a show-off. And he knew it!

Robin threw a rope over to his friend. 'Tie them Roy.'

Roy quickly dismounted and worked his way round the silent soldiers. He bound the rope hard around their wrists, gathering the men up into a tight mass of frightened bodies.

Marian jumped down from the cart and beckoned Robin to one side. 'The village has been starved. The disease has gone, but the Sheriff has not lifted the quarantine. He wants the village for accommodation.'

'And what was your plan?' asked Robin, intrigued. 'To sweet-talk the guards?'

Marian pulled a face. Unfortunately the outlaw was right.

Robin couldn't resist a smug chuckle. 'Bad idea.'

'Oh, and you have better one?'

To Marian's shock, Robin undid his scarf, opening his jerkin to reveal a tiny baby strapped to his chest.

'Here, take this, his name is Seth.' Robin handed

the baby to Marian and then started to stride towards the barricaded village gates.

'Nobody goes in there. Sheriff's orders.' Peter was shouting now, kicking and bucking at his bonds.

The direct challenge was too irresistible for words. Robin doffed an imaginary cap and respectfully stepped back again, manoeuvring towards the cart. 'Very well my friend!'

Peter looked down for an instant, then felt a rush of air above him. An arrow was soaring over the Sheriff's men into the Clun enclosure.

'Why you…' The sergeant began to swear.

Robin's arrow was skewered with a generous loaf of fresh bread.

Inside the village confines, a peasant heard a dull thud outside his cottage door. The malnourished man crumpled with relief when he discovered the loaf sitting on his doormat. Like manna from heaven, food began to gently rain down on his neighbours. Bewilderment turned into joy as the families began to eat for the first time in weeks.

'That is a waste of arrows.' Marian cuddled the baby into her so that Robin wouldn't be able to see that she was annoyed with the way he was showing off and having so much fun. Deep down inside herself, however, Marian was secretly smiling – this behaviour was so Robin, and something she had once admired him for. Robin and Roy had been firing arrows for half an hour now, and were thoroughly enjoying their new-found sport.

'No...' Robin shook his head in mock reproach. This Marian with the new 'attitude' was something Robin was finding hard to understand. Things had been very different five years ago.

'You could simply throw the food.'

Robin appeared to consider the idea for a moment. 'You could, but where would be the fun in that?'

Marian's retort was interrupted by a distant cry from inside the village walls.

'God bless you, Robin Hood!'

Robin nodded gallantly and loaded his bow with a particularly large beef pie.

'This was my idea.' Marian hated behaving like a petulant child, but why did Robin always have to steal the glory?

Roy speared a pair of apples with an arrow. He was feeling awful. Performing such a good deed with Robin, only served to highlight how terrible the thing was that he was planning to do later. By killing Robin he would effectively end the doing of this kind of good deed forever.

Suddenly Marian was screaming. 'Robin!?'

Robin flinched in pain as something struck him. He looked down to find an arrow embedded deep in his arm, his sleeve already soaked in blood.

CHAPTER EIGHT

Peter dropped his bow and began to untie his men. It had taken many agonising minutes with his pocket blade to shear off the cord binding his arms. He'd nearly severed his wrist in the frantic struggle to get free, but the sergeant was unswerving in his task. Robin Hood was not going to get away with mocking the law on his turf.

'Come on!' Peter barked at the first soldier to stand free, thrusting his bow back into his arms. The soldier reached for his quiver, took aim and then bombarded the outlaws with arrows at point blank range.

Marian and Roy instinctively ducked their heads at the onslaught, although their eyes remained focussed on Robin. Robin forced himself to take another look at the wound and realised that he had to act fast. Closing his eyes, he took in a deep breath and then twisted and drew the arrow back out. Roy winced and turned away, the pain must be excruciating.

White with shock, Robin steadied himself and reached his good arm out towards Marian. 'Give me the baby.'

Marian shook her head. 'Let me help you.'

'No. Feeding the poor is foolish, but understandable. Helping me is a hanging offence.' Robin reached again for the baby, then suddenly lurched forward to force Marian to the ground.

'Duck!'

A brace of arrows swooped past so close to them that Marian could feel the air whistling above her head. For a moment she allowed herself to rest face-to-face with Robin, the child cradled between them. Marian smiled gratefully, wordlessly acknowledging that yet again she owed him her life.

Robin returned her grin. 'This is dangerous sport for a girl.'

'More than it is for a child?' Marian couldn't help but prickle. 'Is he yours?'

Robin gathered up his wounded arm and reached again for little Seth. Marian whispered a prayer for the child under her breath then swiftly secured the infant back into Robin's jerkin. The baby settled at once, comforted by the feel of the man's heartbeat.

'Robin?' Roy was already mounted on his horse.

It was imperative that the outlaws retreated to the forest before the Sheriff's men were able to rally and make chase.

Somehow Robin managed to swing himself up into the mare's saddle.

'Split up.'

Roy hesitated, torn between an order and his own imperative. 'But – '

'No buts.' Robin wasn't about to have a debate on the subject.

The men disappeared in opposite directions, leaving Marian to blink her eyes in the dust. What was she supposed to do – go home? She slowly walked back towards her own horse, wondering what might become of the men.

Suddenly Marian was forced to steady herself against the cart as the Sheriff's company stormed past on horseback. As he drew level, Peter paused for a moment to survey her from his mount. His eyes were glinting with an eerie resolve, which somehow Marian understood. *This is not the end of it.*

Robin galloped through the undergrowth, directing his horse as best as he could with his good arm. The weight of the child made his wound throb with pain and his sleeve was already growing sticky with blood. As the path curved round the roots of a tree, Robin sensed an indistinct rumble crescendo behind him – the Sheriff's men were gaining on him.

On the other side of the bend, Robin's horse emerged without its rider. Robin had sunk onto the damp earth and was crawling forward underneath the ferns. Panting with exhaustion, he had to virtually drag the baby under him to make cover in time.

Suddenly a thunder of horses' hooves pounded past them. The baby squawked in response to the deafening noise, its little arms flailing out of its swaddle.

'Sshh. Don't forget the last man.' Robin gently put his finger in the baby's mouth and held his breath. Thankfully the child began to suckle as the last horse clattered round the bend then slowed to a trot.

Robin attempted vainly to peer through the stems, but it was impossible. The trotting horse circled and slowed to a stop just short of the ferns. Discovery could only be seconds away.

Robin could feel the blood pumping out of his arm and was suddenly consumed by a wave of nausea. He gritted his teeth in concentration, then silently

reached for his short sword. It would soon be time to fight for himself and the baby, even though his chances were poor.

The wait was agonising.

Just when Robin couldn't bear it a moment longer, the tip of a blade parted the ferns above him. Robin looked up to face his executioner… and saw Roy.

'Where did you get that dagger?' Robin scolded, smiling with relief. 'And announce yourself next time – I might have killed you.'

Roy stood rooted to the spot, while his friend rolled out of the bracken.

'Have we lost them?'

'We are alone.' Roy's voice was rasping, fraught.

Robin stooped to look at the baby. 'I said split up. You disobeyed me. But I am glad that you did.'

Roy tightened the grip on his dagger, his eyes fixed on Robin.

'It will soon be dark. Our mission to reunite mother and child should wait a day.' Robin winced as he patted the torn cloth around his arrow wound. 'What do you think?'

'It cannot wait.'

Robin looked up, confused. 'Why not?'

'Robin, I am sorry…' Tears pricked Roy's eyes

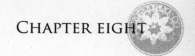

as he raised the dagger, ready to drive it into his friend's heart.

CHAPTER NINE

'Robin?'

Roy immediately dropped the dagger to his side and reeled around on his boot. Marian was just a few feet away from them, gathering her skirts in one hand as she lowered herself out of her saddle. Almost delirious with his own treachery, Roy backed away into the foliage.

Marian quickly followed and crouched down next to Robin, gently raising his arm so she could examine it properly. When she glanced up she was irritated to discover that his friend was still lurking in the branches, gawping at them.

'Don't just stand there.'

Roy swallowed and nodded. *He had to pull himself together.*

While Marian comforted the baby and discussed the situation with Robin, Roy fetched the horses. His hands were shaking so badly when he reached for his mare's bridle, he was forced to hold them behind his back.

'You know who I am?'

A young woman opened the croft door then curtsied at once.

'Lady Marian.'

Marian knew she was well-respected by Knighton folk, many of them remembered the good days when her father was once the Sheriff. Now she was banking on their favour.

'No. You have not seen me, understood?' Her answer came in a half-whisper.

Marian's eyes darted to the hay bales stacked up in the barn next door. Robin, Roy and the baby were all hiding somewhere in the straw, just a stone's throw away from them.

The farm girl, Tess, nodded at the noblewoman, mature enough not to show her surprise. 'As you wish.'

Marian smiled gratefully. 'Can you help me? Do you have a needle and thread, and a little milk?'

Within moments Tess was ushering the odd party into the cosy shelter of the barn, before running back out to fetch water and milk for the baby. Robin and Roy knew this could only be a temporary sanctuary, but it was welcome nonetheless.

Marian sat on a milking stool in the croft and turned Robin's lame arm towards a stream of sunlight flooding in through a hole in the thatch. The wound was deep and sorely needed stitching.

'This needle is thick and blunt. Are you prepared?'

Robin laughed half-heartedly. 'It's the way you sell it.'

'You'll have to take off your…' Marian lowered her eyes and gestured to Robin's shirt. She made a show of concentrating on threading the needle, leaving him free to undress. When Marian turned back to face him, her eyes were drawn to a dark scar on Robin's chest.

The scar was a sober testimony of Robin's years fighting for Richard in the Holy Land. 'Saracen attack on the King. Caught us unawares,' he explained. 'To this day, I do not know how.'

Marian was intrigued. 'Is this why you returned?'

Robin nodded. 'The stitching became infected. I took a fever. When I awoke, the King had moved south and left orders that I should recover fully.'

'So you return and take instantly to the woods?'

Robin remained silent – he was too tired to fight now. He watched as Marian soaked a cloth in her hand bowl, flinching as she bathed his arm.

'It must be clean or you will take with another fever.'

Robin squeezed his fists together and tried to take his mind off things with some light conversation.

'So you never told me, in the years that I was away in the Holy Land… you have had suitors?' Marian pushed the needle into Robin's arm, causing the discussion to degenerate into a yelp of pain.

'I must have.'

The colour drained from Robin's face as Marian pulled the needle through and out the other side. She moved up a fingernail, then punctured the skin to make another stitch. Robin gripped onto Marian's other arm, and tried again.

'It is surprising that you are not married.'

Marian smiled patiently. 'It is. And yet, when one considers that marriage requires a *man*, perhaps not.'

Robin tipped his head to one side and grinned rakishly at Marian.

'A word of advice. Your charms, such as they are, ceased working on me at least five years ago.'

'A challenge,' decided Robin with relish.

'A statement.' Marian tugged the thread back out

and shook her head. She couldn't forgive Robin for leaving her all that time ago, not yet. He'd chosen the glory of a foreign war over her love and a life with his people – it was too late to go back now.

'Ouch!' Robin winced and grasped his elbow.

'That hurt?'

'Yes.'

'Good.' Marian grinned to herself as she pulled the last stitch through. 'Just tying off.'

Robin assumed the face of a choirboy. 'Kiss it better?'

A scream echoed from the rafters of the dusty barn. Marian had been careful to make sure that the stitches were tied off nice and tight.

'You spying? Up to no good?'

Roy sprung away from the door and turned to face the farm girl. He could feel the dagger glinting in his pocket and wished he could just get this over with.

Tess laughed conspiratorially then carried her tray into the barn.

'Explain the child.' Marian was standing with her hands on her hips, as Robin gently rocked the baby back and forth.

'Foundling. We are returning him to his mother.' Robin blushed when he saw Tess enter the room.

'Sorry, heard crying. This is the milk and...' Tess paused and looked at Marian, '...cheese for the mother.'

There was an uncomfortable silence.

'This is not... this is not our child,' said Marian. For less than a second, she held Robin's gaze in a moment of regret. A horse whinnied out in the yard and the pair were distracted by Much's voice, grumbling about something or other. Robin handed over the baby and headed for the door.

'Stay here.'

When Robin returned, Marian was kissing the baby's face and whispering nursery rhymes. He stood watching her for a moment, picturing the life he could never have with her – as his wife, as the mother of his children. As she turned her beautiful face towards him he noticed that it was clouded with anger.

'Can you take the baby? Its mother is in Knighton.'

Marian looked up at once. 'Me? What, because I'm a woman?'

'Because I must go. My men are here.'

'Hmm… the call of the wild.' Marian flicked her hair away from her face in irritation.

Robin sighed. 'Marian. Why is it that everything you say sounds like a criticism?'

'I do not know. I suppose these are the lives we've chosen.' Marian gestured out to the commotion in the yard. 'Always different directions.'

'And you think your direction is better?'

The noblewoman looked down at her expensive robes and trinkets, then nodded. 'I work within the system. It's the only way.'

Robin chuckled. 'Not at night. You dress up as… who is it? The Nightwatchman.'

Marian gritted her teeth – she couldn't bear it when he tried to belittle her like this. When the Sheriff's spies gave up their watch at midnight, Marian had been known to disguise herself and take to the streets. It was the only way she could practically help the poor without risking her father's safety. 'I do not taunt the Sheriff. I do not publicly flout his decisions.'

Robin rubbed his chin in confusion. 'Today, at Clun?'

'That was different,' Marian frowned. 'An emergency.'

Robin flashed his eyes appreciatively. 'You were wonderful. I wish there more emergencies...'

Marian could feel herself bristling. 'Is it all a joke for you?'

'Is it all so serious for you?'

'Forgive me for being careful, but so far nobody has had their *tongue* cut out because of me!' Marian's voice had risen to a shout, as she paced across the croft floor.

Robin was stung. His defiant return to Locksley had unwittingly placed several of his people in danger from the Sheriff, and he felt guilty for it everyday.

'Keep your baby.'

Marian thrust Seth into Robin's chest and stormed out of the barn.

By the time Robin followed her out, she had saddled up and gone. His men stood in the doorway of the barn, subdued by the outburst.

Tess leant out of the hay store. 'A storm's coming from the east. A forest's no place for a bairn. You stay here while you have him.'

Roy was at Robin's elbow. 'No, we can't. There isn't time.'

'Why?' asked Robin.

'We've got to get the baby back to his mother.'

Allan dismissed Roy and looked up to the inviting warmth of the croft. 'Do it tomorrow.'

Roy bit his lip and imagined what his mother was going through tonight. She only had until sunrise, but what could he do?

Oblivious, Much smiled hopefully. 'Perhaps when storms come in future, we could use this barn again?'

Robin shook his head. 'It's dangerous for Tess if we're found here.'

'But what if it's really wet?' Much had to press.

Allan raised his eyes. 'What if you're really wet?'

The farm girl cut the conversation short. 'You'd best get inside and not be seen. All of you. I want you gone before dawn.'

Much was first in the doorway. 'I gather there was some cheese…?'

After much chiding and laughter the company followed him inside. Only Roy hung back in the yard, sweating anxiously as he desperately tried to calculate his next move.

•

CHAPTER TEN

It was a weary ride back to Knighton Hall. As the cart trundled along the lane skirting Sherwood Forest, Marian felt drained and very alone. Robin was infuriating, but he was at least an ally – who could tell when their paths would cross again?

Marian heartened when she turned into her own valley and spotted the smoke from the household's fire curling up towards the evening sky. She guided the cart into the stables and quietly threw some hay down for the pony. As she looked across the cobbled yard however, her heart froze. Two black destrier horses were tethered to the mounting block, tacked up in the Sheriff's ceremonial livery.

At once fearing for her father's safety, Marian brushed down her gown and made her way towards the house.

The Sheriff of Nottingham stepped out of the front door to greet her, flanked by Gisborne and the young sergeant, Peter. It was hardly a surprise. Marian straightened her back and acknowledged each man with a proud smile. Inside, she was in turmoil.

'Marian?' Sir Edward stepped forward to lead his daughter into the house. His face was ashen, telling Marian in an instant everything she needed to know. This was trouble. *Big* trouble.

For once, Sheriff Vaizey decided to dispense with any pleasantries.

'Rumours abound. People are saying that the pestilence is over.'

Marian was cool. 'It is over.'

'My dear, that was between you and me and the Council of Nobles.' He stretched back in her father's chair, resting his boots on the grate of the fireplace. 'Now we have a problem. Either I say that you were wrong, that you made a mistake and we leave the quarantine in place…'

'I was *not* wrong,' Marian could not stop herself from cutting in. Her father stood behind her chair, anxiously holding onto the carved headrest. Marian could not afford to challenge the Sheriff – he would order their death warrant at the merest whim. Sir Edward knew that breaking his silence would only make things worse – all he could do was pray.

The Sheriff paused and weighed up Marian's

statement. 'I could say that you were right and lift the quarantine, let the layabouts live and find somewhere else to house my garrison.'

'Then say that I was right.'

The Sheriff's eyes twinkled. 'There is a catch. In politics there is always a trade. If I say that you were right, then I lose face. That cannot be. We must have authority. I would have to punish you. For your outspokenness.'

Marian stiffened. 'Punish me?!'

The Sheriff leant forward in his seat to face Marian, but turned his eyes to Peter. 'I do not listen to suggestions that you were consorting with Robin Hood. That would be unforgivable.'

Marian couldn't bring herself to look up at the sergeant's smug face. The intensity of the conversation was crushing – she couldn't bear for the men to be in the house a moment longer.

'What punishment?'

'Nothing personal, you understand. Just politics. But it would have to hurt.' The Sheriff stood up to admire a portrait of her mother.

Marian coldly repeated the question. 'What punishment?'

It was to be a public event.

The Sheriff's staff ushered a curious throng of townspeople into the castle courtyard. The men and women filed into the square, sombre-faced at the sight of the gallows. No one was cheering – the atmosphere in Nottingham of late had grown too nervy. If the daughter of the old Sheriff could be punished, no one was safe. Neighbour was suspecting neighbour across the length and breadth of the shire.

A loud clatter of bolts heralded Marian's entrance through the great door of the castle dungeon. Her face remained unmoved, but her appearance was immediately shocking. Dressed only in a sackcloth, the guards had untied her hair so that it tumbled free down her back. Flanked by two hulking jailers coarsely prodding her towards the gallows, Marian's nobility and title were reduced to nothing.

The Sheriff smiled with satisfaction as he watched from the upper gallery. Gisborne and Edward were sat beside him, each man subdued by their own internal monologue.

As Marian shook her hair out of her eyes, the Sheriff winked conspiratorially at his Man At Arms. 'Long and Flowing. Pretty.'

Marian slowly climbed the gallows, her face still composed, even haughty. It was the Sheriff's cue to stand up and address his people.

'We cannot have challenges to our authority. The law applies to us all,' he gestured towards Marian, 'even the privileged.'

An edgy silence sank over the crowd as the Sheriff nodded to the soldier gripping Marian's wrists. The man turned and pushed Marian's head forward with a crude brutality she had never encountered before. It was an act of absolute disrespect. Marian resisted the push, raising her eyes to the Sheriff in wilful defiance.

Sir Edward turned to Gisborne in desperation. Gisborne had never hidden his fondness for Marian, but he could do nothing for her now. Instead his eyes focussed on a spot in front of the gallows, black gloves wringing on his lap.

When the Sheriff's man shoved Marian down for the second time, she decided to succumb. With her head tilted forward, the soldier drew his short sword and began to hack at her hair. Whole clumps were shorn off and scattered onto the crowd, the young woman's head dragged left and right with the swipes of the blade.

The crowd recoiled where the hair fell, unanimously repelled.

When Marian raised her head again, the full intensity of the assault was almost intolerable to Sir Edward. He struggled to fight back the tears, shielding his face in the tapestry behind him.

'Ahh... all that beauty wasted.' The Sheriff felt heady with power. He turned to share his pleasure with Gisborne, but was acknowledged with a rather disappointing nod of the head. Even his Man At Arms was finding it difficult to see merit in this latest violation.

CHAPTER ELEVEN

Much snuffled peacefully and turned over in the straw. He threw an arm across Allan and cuddled up against the warmth of his back. Even in sleep his face appeared to be smiling, overjoyed at the rare luxury of stretching out under thatch. Allan stirred, groaned at the sight of Much dribbling over his shoulder and hauled him off. He pulled his cloak tighter round him then settled back down to his own dreams.

Roy crouched against the croft wall, watching over the sleeping men. He'd been awake all night, rocking backwards and forwards in tortuous repetition as his mind played out every dreadful scenario waiting for him in the morning.

Robin lay at Roy's feet, the tiny infant still curled up against his chest. He was sleeping fitfully, trapped in a twisted rerun of the terrible attack he'd witnessed in the Holy Land. Vicious enemies had broken into King Richard's inner enclosure, forcing Robin to fight for his life. His nightmare was filled with the ghostly wailing song of evening prayer and a barrage of haunting images from that fateful night. He could see the billowing silk of the tent, a flash of steel in the moonlight and then the Saracen, right there, running at him. Thrashing scimitars suddenly appeared at all sides, closing in on Robin. Sensing no escape, Robin felt the cold slice of a blade across his chest. Suddenly he screamed out loud, his cry mingling with the chanting outside... and the screaming baby in the croft.

Robin jolted and opened his eyes. Instead of a Saracen, Roy was somehow looming above him, ready to plunge an assassin's knife into Robin's heart.

'Roy?'

Roy pushed the dagger down on his friend. 'Sorry.'

Robin woke up fast. Letting the baby roll to the side, he pushed back on the blade with all his energy. Both men strained, but Robin was stronger. In one deft move, he threw Roy off, sending him tumbling across the floor. Terrified and disorientated, Roy scrambled to his feet only to be tackled and wrestled back to the ground. Robin kneeled on his attacker's chest, nursing his injured arm.

'What are you doing?' Robin was shouting now, allowing himself to take on board the betrayal. 'What are you doing!'

Much, Will and Allan were finally roused by the struggling men. There was a flurry of shadows as they each leapt across the wooden boards to restrain Roy. Past the point of any return, Roy bucked and fought with all his might.

'…kill him …I've got to kill him!'

Robin started to shake the boy. 'We came to rescue you! Every man here was ready to risk his life for you!'

The men dragged Roy to his feet. As they held him upright he surrendered completely, allowing himself to hang in their arms. Robin drew back his fist to hit him in the jaw, then dropped it down again.

'In a war, a rescued man owes his life to his rescuers. He gives his life like *that*,' Robin clicked his fingers, 'to the men that saved him.'

Roy panted, limp with emotion.

'What is this?' Little John climbed up from his bunk in the haystack below, his question echoing round the darkened loft.

Much shook his head. 'This one tried to kill Robin.'

98

Roy was so overwhelmed with shame, he could hardly lift his head.

'You were my son.' John stepped back into the eaves, his face contorted with disgust. Then all at once he was amongst them again, thundering across the floor to deliver a terrible punch. Roy was sent flying into the wall, backing away in terror as the man charged back to strike him again.

'No! John!' Robin pulled John off Roy before he battered him.

'Kill me.' Roy's request was totally sincere.

'I will kill you.' Little John towered above the lad, overcome with fury.

'No!' Robin was starting to see things clearly. 'I am trying to think. Let me think.'

John stepped away from the boy, leaving Roy to collapse weeping to the floor.

Robin crouched down and rested his hand on Roy's shoulder. 'What have I ever done to you that would make you want to kill me?'

'Just kill me.' Roy closed his eyes and turned to the wall.

'No.'

'My mother,' Roy whispered. 'They have my mother.'

Robin patted his friend on the shoulder and recognised the pain in his eyes for the first time. 'And they will kill her unless you kill me first?'

'She will die at sunrise.'

The croft fell silent as the company contemplated the impossible scenario.

Will spoke first. 'I hate the Sheriff.'

Robin was starting to recap on the implications of the last few days. 'And the story of the baby's mother, that was a lie too?'

'Gisborne is the father.'

'Gisborne?' Will was incredulous.

'The mother is a kitchen girl. She thinks Gisborne took her child to Kirklees Abbey, to be raised there.'

Will sucked through his teeth — that was pretty low, even for the Man At Arms. 'I hate Gisborne too.'

Much dragged Roy up by his shirt. 'That doesn't mean this one can go round killing my master.'

'Roy had to kill me or see his mother die. Which would you choose?' asked Robin.

Much grumbled petulantly and stared down at the toes poking out of his careworn stockings. 'I have no mother.'

'Roy does. Come on.' Robin sprung up with a renewed energy – it was time to take action.

'What?' Much hated having this type of conversation in the middle of the night. Skipping meals was one thing, but to be deprived of sleep was almost too much to bear.

Robin looked round at each of the party, then bent down to scoop up baby Seth. 'Now we have two mothers to rescue before sunrise.'

CHAPTER TWELVE

The castle guards whispered under their breath and stamped their feet in the chill of the early morning darkness. When the dairy cart rolled up to the gates, they sauntered over to share a joke with the farmer. The cart was laden with pitchers of milk, still warm from the cow. After five minutes the farmer remounted and waved as the guards beckoned him through.

The steady shire horse found its own way under the stone arch and into the castle courtyard. It had walked the route a thousand times before. As the cart drew up in the gloomy half-light, a concealed wooden hatch dropped open to expose Allan and Will. The men clambered out of their hiding place and set down onto the cobbles. Allan flicked a silver coin over to the farmer and in an instant the pair had disappeared.

The guards at the gates were sitting ducks. Allan and Will approached them from behind, knocking each one unconscious with a controlled blow to the head. Will stepped forward and gestured through the mist to Robin and the rest of the men.

Soon the whole company were standing in the shadows of the castle courtyard. As they approached the side flanked by the dungeon, each man was arrested by the sight of the scaffold. The grim wooden structure was a gruesome presence in the half-light – Roy couldn't even bear to look. Little John gripped his arm in silent support, but the lad was distracted by the morning sky. It was not yet dawn, but an aura of light was already starting to glow above the turrets.

'Hurry,' urged Roy. 'It is nearly dawn. They'll be making her ready.'

They knew what had to be done. The main party noiselessly made its way towards the cloisters, whilst Allan lifted a basket of eggs from the milk cart and set off alone.

Within minutes Robin was face-to-face with the solid oak door leading down to the dungeons. It seemed impenetrable, but Will unbuckled the sheath of tools strapped to his chest and set to work on the hinges.

While Will worked and guided the bolts, Allan strolled into the castle kitchens. Cooks pulled loaves

out of the fire while the serving girls weaved in amongst them laying platters ready for breakfast. Allan quickly sighted a maiden that matched Roy's description and made his way towards her.

'Annie? This belongs to you.' Instead of eggs, Allan held out the velvet shawl.

Annie reached for the shawl and clasped it tight to her. She could smell him – she could still smell her baby. When the shawl finally came away from her cheeks, Allan winced to see the grief wracking her young face.

Without torches, the dungeon corridors were almost as black as pitch. Rats crept amongst them as Roy led the way through the damp passageways, cursing until he finally reached the network of cells underneath the castle.

'Mother!' Roy grasped the bars of the first chamber and peered into its foul depths. When there was no response he began to sob, tormented by the unrelenting slipping of time.

'Mary? Mary?' shouted Robin, stepping up the company's efforts as they quickly moved from cell to cell. It was a labyrinth, *how could they ever hope to find her?*

Suddenly torches flared at the far end of the corridor. Roy was at first blinded by the light, then dismayed to see the Sheriff, Gisborne and a troop of their men gathered up ahead. They had been waiting for him.

The Sheriff was alive with delight as he aped Robin's concern. 'Mary? Mary?'

'Where is she?' demanded Roy. 'What have you done with her?'

The Sheriff stared out of the thin opening gouged into the castle wall. Past him, the burnt orange of the sun was just beginning to glow above the horizon.

'What do you think Gisborne? Does that look like first light to you?'

Gisborne stepped forward and nodded, savouring the buzz of control.

Roy's eyes were locked on Robin, unable to accept that his mother's fate was truly sealed.

The Sheriff addressed Roy darkly. 'I kept my side of the bargain. You didn't keep yours.'

An unnatural cry of fury came from Roy's body as he made a lunge for the Sheriff and Gisborne. He was still kicking and spitting like a madman as Robin fought to restrain him. At last Little John clasped two colossal arms around the lad's chest, dragging him

back a pace.

The Sheriff turned away from the skirmishing outlaws to address his commanding officer. The order was brutal and explicit.

'Bring them with us to see "Mary, Mary" swing.'

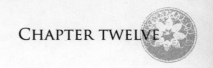

CHAPTER THIRTEEN

'Do you want a hood?' The hangman's voice was business-like, practical. When he didn't get a response, he stooped down to catch the tiny old woman's preference.

Mary White was shaking with terror. She gazed at the hangman blankly, before lowering her head in a weak nod. She looked unbearably alone in the empty courtyard, a horribly inappropriate candidate for a lonely death on the gallows.

'Mother!'

Roy and the outlaws emerged from the cloisters, flanked by the Sheriff and Gisborne.

The Sheriff stepped up to the scaffold and clicked his tongue thoughtfully at the Hangman as if he was picking out what to have for breakfast.

'No hood, I think.'

Roy's voice was hoarse with distress. 'You will rot in hell for this.'

'Only this?' The Sheriff raised his arms in mock alarm, then turned back to the gallows. 'Mary, Mary's boy's contrary, time to see her swing.'

'Murderers!' A piercing woman's voice tore through the half-light. 'I will kill you!'

It was Annie, wild-eyed with rage, her hair blowing in the morning breeze. She was wielding a huge kitchen knife in her right hand, holding it fiercely up to Guy of Gisborne's neck.

The Man At Arms spoke calmly. 'Annie…'

'Do not move!' Annie pulled the blade towards her so that its edge pressed against Gisborne's Adam's apple. 'You said he would be safe. You left him in the woods. You left him to *die*. Our son! Our baby!'

'Gisborne! Tut, tut!' The Sheriff reproved, chuckling at the indiscretion. The morning had turned out to be gold star entertainment. He stole a look at Robin – his presence never failed to up the ante.

Two sergeants approached the serving girl, swords still resting in their scabbards. In a trice she flashed the meat cleaver away from Gisborne and raised it above them, stopping the men in their tracks.

Robin saw his chance. Bracing his wounded arm, he elbowed the two men at his sides. As they collapsed, winded, he kneed them for good measure and seized their weapons. He then leapt up onto the wooden boards of the scaffold, kicking the hangman

to the floor.

Annie renewed her grip on Gisborne, using her free hand to clutch him by the hair. Around her the rest of the men threw themselves into bitter hand-to-hand conflict. Much pitched his trusty shield against two armed soldiers as he dragged himself up the side of the scaffold, then brought it down mercilessly on their heads. Will ripped and tore with his hand axe, cutting a bloody path as he paced his way through the Sheriff's troops.

In the midst of the fighting Gisborne suddenly swung round to smash Annie's face with his clenched fist. As she staggered back the knife fell onto the stones, but Allan stepped across to guide her away from the scaffold.

Little John swiped at the hangman with one easy movement, then stepped forward to pick up Mary. He carefully lifted the old lady down from the gallows, as Robin's company fought their way backwards to the castle gate.

'To the horses.' Robin barked his order, then turned to follow the men.

'Locksley!'

Robin stopped.

'Why so hasty my friend?' The Sheriff stood in

the middle of the courtyard, clutching the assassin's dagger to Roy's throat.

Roy's eyes bulged in panic as the Sheriff dragged him back against the stone wall of the cloisters.

'Sorry to spoil your day, but go and he gets it.'

Robin was torn in half.

The Sheriff's gaze was full of understanding. 'It's our old friend the dilemma again.'

He was a far more brutal hostage-taker than Annie. He crushed the short blade so deep into Roy's neck, the boy began to cough and gasp for air.

Much tugged at Robin's cuff. 'Master…'

Robin stared past his manservant to Mary White, her cloudy eyes pleading for the life of her son.

'You cannot give yourself up every five minutes.' Much's tone was firm, desperate.

Roy drew a breath. 'Robin, no!'

'Robin, yes!' The Sheriff was loving the drama.

The outlaw pulled an arrow from his quiver and set it in his bow in a deliberate, open-handed movement. He held his breath then focussed the dart on the Sheriff's forehead.

'Let him go. Or we will all die today.'

The Sheriff smiled patiently. 'Robin we have had this conversation, and we both know that you are

not really the killing type.'

Robin's answer was to slowly pull back the taut string of the bow. This time he meant it.

Roy watched the archer prepare to fire – *could all this death, all this bloodshed really have come about because of him?*

In that split second, Roy overcame all the dilemmas. Before Robin could release his arrow, Roy let out an animalistic howl and pulled himself free of the Sheriff. He snatched the dagger from the Sheriff's hand and pointed it into his ribs.

'Run, Robin!' Roy was insistent. 'For my mother. For the baby.'

He ripped the dog tag from his neck and hurled it towards Little John. John's heart was breaking as he took a last look at the boy who had been like a son to him. But he knew he had to be strong and as he turned away he carefully tucked Roy's tag into his pocket and then guided Mary further away.

'No! Roy!'

Roy was oblivious to his mother's frantic cry. He swiped his blade indiscriminately at the Sheriff and the throng of soldiers that were circling in on him. The gesture bought valuable time, but only seconds. Roy was knocked to his knees by a sword blow to the side, swiftly followed by another.

'My name is Royston White, and I fight for Robin Hood and King Richard.' Roy's voice sailed out to his retreating comrades, strong and proud and true.

Robin took aim again, desperately searching for a clear line of sight. As he focussed, the hangman staggered towards him swinging a broad timber left and right. Robin ducked to avoid the wood. When he rose again he could see that he was too late for Roy. His friend disappeared behind a battery of soldiers, sinking under a sea of blows.

Little John was careful to shield Mary's view as he led her towards the castle gate.

'He does this for you,' he whispered hoarsely. 'Come. Live.'

CHAPTER FOURTEEN

Peter and his men had been toiling at Clun for half a day already. As the troops sweated to dismantle the barricade encircling the village, their young sergeant barked with irritation at every approach. Clun was being liberated and nothing seemed to please him less.

A gaunt band of villagers huddled together to watch the wattle fence finally come down. So many had already perished, it was hard to believe the nightmare might be over.

Peter pulled open an official proclamation and started to read in a monosyllabic tone. 'The Sheriff of Nottingham hereby announces that the quarantine has been successful in preventing the spread of this heinous disease. The restriction of movement order is hereby lifted and the Sheriff thanks the people of Clun for their patience.'

Marian took this as her cue to order her driver to urge her cart forward. For a second time it was laden with provisions, but today the cart was uncovered –

there for all to see. When the barricades were finally pulled away, the villagers made their first tentative steps towards the noblewoman. Soon the cart was surrounded by hungry men, women and children, finally being given the chance to live.

The Sheriff's men finished up, then prepared to ride back to Nottingham Castle. Peter rose in his saddle as he passed Marian's cart, shooting her a look of utter contempt. Marian held her head high and returned his glare with an equally steady gaze. Her hair had been roughly hacked off to her shoulders and her head looked fragile and damaged in the sunshine, but she would never let him see the humiliation that still made her smart each time she saw herself in a looking glass.

'Not stopping for a pie?'

Peter's face was sour as he led his men away.

Annie waited by the leafy track, cradling Seth over her shoulder. The baby was content, cooing and gurgling against his mother's neck as she chatted to Robin and his men. Around noon Marian cantered up to greet the group. She was accompanied by a stable lad from her household, driving the empty cart.

It was time for Annie and her baby to make a new start – far, far away from the dangers of Nottingham. The outlaws mooched under the trees, waiting to say their goodbyes.

'Your hair?' Robin was startled.

Marian shrugged disinterestedly. 'It was a nuisance to wash.'

Annie stepped forward and curtsied respectfully to her. 'Thank you my Lady. I do not know how to…'

Marian waved her hand dismissively. 'Lady Glasson is a good mistress, and you will be well-provided for. Seth too.'

Annie turned to Robin and his men. 'Thank you. From me. And especially from…'

As she held Seth up, Robin gave him an affectionate squeeze on the cheek. The baby broke into a spontaneous smile. Seth's sweet toothless grin was infectious, heartening the entire company.

'Go,' urged Marian. 'You have a long journey.'

Will stepped forward and bashfully handed Annie a small leather pouch. 'One thing – we er – open it later.'

'Thank you.' Annie climbed onto the cart and set her sights on the horizon.

As they waved the brave new family off, Little John remained silent. It had been the second goodbye in two days. He remembered the funeral pyre they had burnt in Roy's honour last sunset and the pain that tore across him when he'd surrendered the lad's wooden mace to the flames. Mary's farewell gift to her son had been a single rose. John had stayed close to the pyre long after it had burnt away, thinking about the boy they had lost – *him I liked.*

Now, turning Roy's dog tag in his large hand, John said quietly, and to no one in particular, 'I will never forget you lad. I will always wear your tag with pride, in your honour.'

'I am going this way,' Marian circled her horse and pointed up the track.

Robin tilted his head towards Sherwood Forest. 'I am going…'

'I know. Always different directions.' Marian smiled wanly, then spurred her horse towards home.

Robin watched her silhouette fade until it had shrunk to nothing, then signalled for the men to retreat beneath the canopy of trees. One-by-one the band disappeared into the undergrowth, striking out for their camp in the heart of the forest.

'I will not miss that baby,' confessed Much, as his

horse clopped lazily through a birch wood.

Will grinned. 'Me neither.'

'Peace!'

'Sleep,' added Allan.

Much sighed wistfully. '*Sleeves* on my tunic.'

Epilogue

Annie gently nursed Seth to sleep then swaddled him to her, as the cart trundled through Nottingham's meadows and pastures. This was the most important journey of her life, a whole new start with the child she had believed she could never know. As she bathed in the warmth of the afternoon sun, Annie reached down for Will's gift. She opened the leather bag and at once laughed. Inside was a miniature wooden bow and quiver set, just the thing for a tiny outlaw-in-training..